Glamour girls

The English Roses

Runway Rose

CALLAWAY ARTS & ENTERTAINMENT

19 FULTON STREET, FIFTH FLOOR, NEW YORK, NEW YORK 10038

PUFFIN BOOKS

Published by the Penguin Group
Penguin Young Readers Group, 345 Hudson Street, New York, New York 10014, U.S.A.
Penguin Group (Canada), 90 Eglinton Avenue East, Suite 700, Toronto, Ontario,
Canada M4P 2Y3 (a division of Pearson Penguin Canada Inc.)

Penguin Books Ltd., Registered Offices: 80 Strand, London WC2R 0RL, England

First published in the United States of America by Callaway Arts & Entertainment and Puffin Books, 2009

1   3   5   7   9   10   8   6   4   2

First Edition

Produced by Callaway Arts & Entertainment

Nicholas Callaway, President and Publisher
John Lee, CEO
Cathy Ferrara, Managing Editor and Production Director
Toshiya Masuda, Art Director
Nelson Gómez, Director of Digital Technology
Amy Cloud, Senior Editor
Bomina Kim, Design Assistant • Krupa Jhaveri, Designer
Ivan Wong, Jr. and José Rodríguez, Production
Jennifer Caffrey, Executive Assistant

Special thanks to Doug Whiteman and Mariann Donato.

Library of Congress Cataloging-in-Publication Data is available.

Puffin Books ISBN 978-0-14-241126-1

Printed in the United States of America

www.madonna.com   www.callaway.com   www.penguin.com/youngreaders

All of Madonna's proceeds from this book will be donated to
Raising Malawi (www.raisingmalawi.org), an orphan-care initiative.

The English Roses

by MADONNA
With Amy Cloud

Runway Rose

PUFFIN
CALLAWAY

New York
2009

illustrated by
jeffrey fulvimari

→ Book 9 ←

Contents

CHAPTER I

Spring Has Sprung

bf4eva

amy   grace   Binah   charlotte   nicole

Th(T)here isn't a doubt in my mind that
you, of all people, must have heard of
the English Roses by now. After all,
anyone who's anyone knows that the
words "English Roses" not only refer
to a specific type of lovely flower but to five of the
coolest, hippest, most rockin' girls on this very

planet. And you, as an in-the-know type of chica, are surely aware that their names are Amy Brook, Grace Harrison, Binah Rossi, Charlotte Ginsberg, and Nicole Rissman.

Our story begins on a Monday afternoon in that most fabulous of seasons: spring.

Amy, Nicole, Binah, and Charlotte were a bright, dizzy blur of leaping legs and flailing arms as they hopped about the bleachers in Hampstead School's football stadium. (I really shouldn't have to tell you that football in this particular case is what you Yanks would call soccer!) The fifth of their fivesome, Grace Harrison, blasted down the field with the ball. She pummeled the ball past the other team's goalie and sent it sailing into the net.

"GOAL FOR HAMPSTEAD!" the ref yelled, and the crowd went wild.

After the game ended, the English Roses waited outside the locker room to congratulate Grace.

"What a match!" Amy said, shaking her head of red curls. "Grace is simply . . ."

"The mostest!" Charlotte finished, hugging her Burberry trench coat closer to her body. "She totally rocks the field!"

Suddenly, the locker room door swung open. Grace's deep brown, almond-shaped eyes sparkled as she playfully bounced over to her friends, slapping them high fives. "Holla, ladies!"

The rest of the Roses looked slightly baffled. Grace had moved to London from Atlanta, Georgia, a few years ago, and they still had to get used to some of her American slang.

"You were amazing out there, Grace!" Binah said, throwing her arm around her friend.

"Yeah," Nicole agreed. "You're so obvi going to be a pro footy player someday!" (By the way, in case you're confused as to the use of "obvi," I should fill you in on this: The English Roses *love* to abbreviate their words. Now, back to our regularly scheduled story.)

"Not if I don't ace the big Walsham game two weeks from now," Grace complained, crinkling her eyes in a way that let her friends know just how very worried she was. "If we don't win, we don't go to finals. And you know what that means!"

The English Roses nodded their heads. The Walsham game was all Grace had been talking about for the past, well, three months! And anyone who knows anything about the English Roses knows that Grace loves football big-style.

"Well," Charlotte said with a mischievous glint in her eyes, "I think you definitely should start prepping for the game right away . . . with an ice cream!"

"Well, I'm out!" Amy said. "Mum told me to be home by six. She said something about a surprise."

"Oooh, surprises are super!" Binah squealed.

"Well, the last surprise turned out to be Stella." Amy giggled. "So, I hope it's nothing that dramatic. I don't think our house could handle another baby right now." Stella was Amy's baby sister. At first, Amy had been nervous about the idea of sharing her mum with a newborn, but one glance at Stella had changed all that. Now Amy cherished every available opportunity to spend time with her little sister.

"Aww . . . how is baby Stella doing?" Binah sighed. An only child whose mother died when she was very young, Binah had always wanted a sibling.

"She's great. Soooo adorable!" Amy gushed. "Well, I'd best be on my way or else Mum is going to murder me!" She waved good-bye and headed home.

Stella
7 months
old...

CHAPTER 2

Omg Omg Omg :)

KewlGrl82: OMG OMG OMG OMG

GracieH: LOL! What up?

KewlGrl82: So the surprise iz super kewl!

GracieH: OMG 4 real?

KewlGrl82: Tot. I get 2 help @ Marks & Spencer Teen Fashion Week!

GracieH: No way! Tot awesome. Ur mom got u the job?

KewlGrl82: Ya. So next 2 weeks after skool I will help out.

GracieH: So a maze! What r u going 2 do?

KewlGrl82: I get 2 style + work w/ modelz. N there iz going 2 b a runway show.

GracieH: OMG, no way! Can ER come?

KewlGrl82: U bet-r! Saturday, 21st.

GracieH: O fudge. No way. Same day as footy game! 1 p.m. on the 21st.

KewlGrl82: But show isn't til 8 p.m.

GracieH: O! Kewl 2 da max! So I can come 2 ur show! :D

KewlGrl82: Ya! I can come 2 ur game!

GracieH: Sweet! OMG I am tot nerv.

KewlGrl82: Don't b!

GracieH: But if I don't become star footy player, will die 4 sure.

KewlGrl82: U know u will do gr8! U r the best player on team!

GracieH: Argh!

TruBluNikl4 signing on

TruBluNikl4: Yo gals. Did u do lit paper yet?

GracieH: LOL. :/ No, Nik! Not due 4 like 3 weeks!

KewlGrl82: Nik, guess what? I get 2 work @ Teen Fashion Week @ Marks & Spencer!

TruBluNikl4: No way! Tot amaze! :D

GracieH: She iz n fashion show 2!

TruBluNikl4: OMG AMY! :o

KewlGrl82: LOL, not n it, but will b b-hind scenez.

TruBluNik14: :O)

KewlGrl82: Ya, am so excited.

GracieH: OK. Gotta practice head butts w/ my bros.

KewlGrl82: Ooh, tell Matt I sed hi! ;)

GracieH: LOL! U r horrible. My bro iz 2 old 4 u.

KewlGrl82: He iz still a hottie patottie.

GracieH: ROFL! C U both n school 2 morrow.

TruBluNik14: Bye, Gracie!

things to say:
- for Reals
- super kewl
- tot awesome
- So amaze
- kewl 2 the max
- tot nerv

CHAPTER 3

Fashion Frenzy

Amy could hardly make it through school the following day. All she could think about was working at Teen Fashion Week! She willed the hours to go by faster, which, of course, only made them drag all the more. (Why, pray tell, does time seem to slow down at the very moment you wish it to speed up the most?) But, at long last, the final bell rang, and Amy was the first one in the coatroom, impatiently pulling on her jacket and stuffing her book bag with ferocious speed. She waved a hasty good-bye to her friends and flew out the door. Her mum was waiting outside in the family sedan to drive her to Marks & Spencer.

When they arrived, the two walked into the department store and took the elevator to the top floor, where the fashion show was to be held. The air was filled with the clanging of saws and hammers as workers busily assembled the runway. Well-dressed women clacked noisily back and forth across the tile in high heels, clutching fat look books stuffed with photos of models. In the corner, a tall, lanky man sporting a pencil-thin mustache waved wildly among a cluster of women so skinny they looked like those insects called walking sticks.

Amy wrinkled her nose. They looked *too* skinny, in her humble opinion. Bony and sickly. *When I'm a famous designer,* Amy thought, *I'm going to use real, normal-sized women as my models.*

As Amy and her mum approached, Amy could hear the lanky man barking orders in a loud, shrill voice. "NO NO NO! That is absolutely NOT the right look. Talk about a two-cent cancan dancer wearing a rucksack. And that model! She's got a face like a bulldog chewing a wasp. No, I want DRAMA. I want GLAMOUR. These girls are teenagers, for blinking heck!"

The man was wearing tight-fitted black pants, a white tank top with a thin leather vest thrown over

it, and a colorful silk scarf wound around his neck. Perched atop his nose were black wire-rimmed glasses that were attached to a chain around his neck. His feet were clad in pointy black boots with silver tips and spurs.

"Nigel, I'd like you to meet my daughter Amy," Amy's mum said warmly. "She's going to be helping you out with Teen Fashion Week. Amy, this is Nigel. He's the store's creative director. He decorates the windows, dresses the mannequins, and pretty much runs the show style-wise."

"Oh my—what a STUNNER!" Nigel gushed, taking Amy's hand and kissing it. "Oh, you must be simply BEATING the young lads off with a stick!"

Amy giggled. "Not exactly," she replied. "It's really nice to meet you."

Amy's mum checked her watch. "Uh-oh, I'm late for a meeting with Harvey."

She rushed off, and Nigel peered down at Amy through his glasses.

"So—" he began.

"I really can't tell you how excited I am to be here," Amy interrupted excitedly. "My biggest dream is to become a fashion designer when I get older. In fact, when you have some time, I'd love to sit down and show you some of my ideas." She motioned toward the sketchbook in her arms.

Nigel smiled tightly. "Sure, sure," he said, waving his hand. "However, right now I'm absolutely DYING for a chai latte." He put his hands on Amy's shoulders and turned her around. "But with soy milk, puh-lease. Real milk gives me a case of the gassies." He brought his hand to his pursed lips in a demure smirk. "Now, the kitchen is THAT way. Run along!"

Amy stuttered. She wasn't sure what she was supposed to do. What on earth was a chai latte?

"But, uh . . ." she stammered. "I'm not exactly sure—"

"Sorry, doll. I'm super-duper busy today. So I need you to go ahead and just figure it out, mmm-kay?" And with that he rushed off.

Amy just stood there awkwardly. Chai latte? What did that have to do with fashion? Only one thing was for sure—she had to figure it out. And fast!

CHAPTER 4

Not a Latte Fun

In the employee kitchen, Amy fumbled with the coffee machine. She knew that Winston, Charlotte's butler, often made Mr. Ginsberg lattes, and it had something to do with coffee. So maybe a chai latte had coffee in it? Amy didn't drink coffee and had no clue as to how to operate a coffee machine. But how hard could it be?

Suddenly, one of the female stick insects bustled into the kitchen and flew past Amy. She knocked into Amy's sketchbook, which was on the counter, sending papers and drawings flying all over the room.

"Could you watch where you put things around here?" the woman asked. "This isn't middle school, okay? People are busy!"

Amy prickled with embarrassment as she picked up the papers. "Um, sorry," she apologized, then hesitated. "Do you by any chance know anything about chai lattes?"

The stick insect poured herself a cup of coffee, tossed in four cubes of sugar, then whirled around on one stiletto heel. "No, I don't. Sorry, I'm late. Gotta fly!" She straightened her high-waisted pencil skirt and promptly clacked out of the room.

Amy felt her chest tighten with indignity. But then she took a deep breath. This was real life, she reminded herself. And moreover, it was not brain surgery.

Amy examined the coffee maker and found a can of coffee grounds next to the machine. She spooned in enough coffee to reach the line at the top. Then she filled the attached container with water and switched the "on" button so that it glowed red. The machine began to gurgle happily. *Ahh*, she thought. *That sounds familiar.*

Picking up her sketchbook and a pencil, she began to draw versions of the skinny fashionista. *Let's put her in something not so severe*, she thought. *Hmmm . . . a ruffle at the hem, maybe?* As usual, when Amy started sketching, she forgot all about where she was and became consumed with the design. Soon, the pleasant gurgle of the coffee machine became a distinctly unhappy wheeze.

"Oh no!" she gasped. The pot began to shake and wiggle, and a sludgy brown liquid poured forth from the top. The pot was overflowing! A coffeelike substance oozed over the countertop and on to the floor. Amy put her hands on her face in dismay. What on earth had she gotten herself into?

CHAPTER 5

Hello, Gorgeous!

introducing: Simon Simmons.

Amy was beside herself. Puddles of coffee water were everywhere, and the pot was still shaking and making an awful racket. To make matters worse, she heard heavy footsteps coming down the hall.

Oh, shoot! she thought. *Please, please, please, don't let it be Nigel!*

A shadow loomed in the doorway. Amy cowered and shut her eyes.

"Hey," a friendly voice echoed. "Need some help here?"

Startled, Amy opened her eyes to behold not Nigel or a stick-thin fashion assistant, but instead a tall, muscular boy with sparkling blue eyes. A smile was playing on his lips.

"Or were you just planning on cleaning the floor with coffee? I hear it's an excellent antibacterial agent."

Amy had to giggle. "Um, actually," she said, nervously playing with her hair, "I was just trying to make a chai laffe. I mean, latte."

"Well, here—let me help you clean this up," the friendly boy offered. He grabbed some paper towels and helped Amy mop up the spilled coffee on

All dolled up

the floor and countertop. *What a cutie-patootie,* she thought dreamily.

After they had cleaned up the coffee, the boy stuck out his hand. "By the way, my name is Simon Simmons. I'm here after school working on the runway."

"Hi, Simon. I'm Amy. I'm helping out with the fashion show."

Simon crinkled his beautiful eyes. "I don't think I've seen you around here before."

"I just started today," Amy admitted. "I'm helping after school, too."

"Well, nice to meet you, Amy."

"Nice to meet you, too," Amy replied. She paused. "You wouldn't happen to know how to make a chai latte, would you?"

Simon scratched his chin in thought. "Hey. Now that you mention it, I think I saw some tea bags somewhere that said 'chai' on them. I wonder if those would help?"

He poked around in one of the cabinets. "A-ha! Here you go," he said, handing Amy a tea bag with CHAI printed neatly on it.

"Thanks a million!" Amy gushed. "This is perfect."

"No problem." Simon smiled, then winked. "Nice meeting you, Amy. See you around."

Amy felt her stomach flutter. Every time he looked at her, she felt like swooning. He was just... the most!

"See you soon!" Amy called after him. *Hopefully real soon*, she thought.

CHAPTER 6

See How
the Cookie Crumbles

ack at fashion central, Nigel was busy with his stick insect army. A towering, willowy fashion model stood in front of them, clad in a smart little plaid mini-dress.

Amy cleared her throat. "Your chai latte is ready, Nigel."

Nigel peered down at her curiously. "What? Oh. Yes. Thank you." He brought the steaming mug to his lips.

PPHHRRFFT. Hot liquid sprayed from Nigel's mouth almost like a fountain—all over the model, the stick insects, and even on Amy herself. Nigel's eyes bugged out of his head like those of a frog in mid-ribbit.

"WHAT IS THIS?" Nigel roared.

"Um, it's a chai latte," Amy said as her stomach fell to somewhere around her knees.

"This is absolutely NOT a chai latte," Nigel fumed. "This . . . this . . . I don't know WHAT to call this. It's sludge! It's filth. It's UNACCEPT-ABLE!"

This outburst proved to be too much, even for a tough cookie like Amy. A pressure that had been building in her chest all afternoon seem to loosen, and her cheeks flushed a deep crimson as she felt her eyes fill with tears. "I'm—I'm sorry," she whispered, then turned and fled the room. This truly was a fashion disaster of the greatest proportions!

CHAPTER 7

Where's Our Amy?

The next day, Amy didn't show up at the usual street corner where the English Roses met to walk to school. The girls waited and waited, until Nicole pointed out that they were going to be late if they didn't start walking.

"I wonder if something bad happened yesterday," Binah worried.

"Maybe they were so impressed with her fashion sense that they gave her a job so she never has to go to school again?!" Charlotte suggested hopefully.

The English Roses' worry mounted when they

arrived at school and Amy had yet to appear. Their worry reached emergency levels when the first bell rang and Amy's seat remained empty.

Finally, just when Mrs. Moss told them to take out their grammar textbooks and begin diagramming sentences, the door opened and in slunk Amy. Only it didn't look like the Amy the English Roses knew so well. Her skin, usually rosy and freckled, was pale. Dark circles hung beneath her usually vibrant green eyes. Her dependably perky smile was nowhere to be seen. And instead of looking like a fashion plate, she was wearing a simple gray T-shirt, jeans, and sneakers. Even her usually bouncy hair seemed less bouncy!

At lunch, Amy told her friends her sad story of the fashion disaster.

"Oh, Amy, I'm so sorry," Binah said, taking her friend's hand in support. "How awful!"

"Winston makes really good chai lattes," Charlotte whispered hopefully. "He might be able to teach you."

"I just don't know what to do," Amy said. "I thought fashion was my thing, but it's obviously not."

"Wait a minute," Grace cut in angrily. "So you can't make a chai latte. Big deal. What does that have to do with fashion anyway?"

Amy thought about it. "Well, nothing," she admitted.

"Right. So, why wouldn't fashion still be your thing? Amy, we all"—she gestured around the cafeteria—"see every day just how talented you are. No one else can put together outfits like you can. Just because some snobby bigwigs treated you badly doesn't change that!"

Amy considered her friend's words. "But I can't go back there," she sniffled. "I can't show my face ever again."

"Maybe you could mention it to your mum?" Nicole suggested. "She could talk to Nigel."

"Absolutely not," Amy insisted. "I don't want to be known as the girl who runs to her mummy every time something doesn't go her way."

"Well, one thing's for certain," Grace said. "You can't let them win. You have to go back and prove to them that you're better than that. You have to try again."

Deep down inside, Amy knew that Grace was

right. But did that mean she really had to face Nigel
and the walking sticks again?

CHAPTER 8

Bet-r 2-day

Charlotte: Hey gurl. How did it go?

KewlGrl82: Bet-r 2-day. But I tot just helped Simon. LOL.

Charlotte: Real-e?:o)

KewlGrl82: Ya, he iz so dreamy! I am tot crushing!

Charlotte: Aw, but isn't he n secondary school?

KewlGrl82: Ya ;)

Charlotte: Well am glad ur day was bet-r.

KewlGrl82: Ya, still freaked by Nigel + stick insects tho.

Charlotte: :(

GracieH signing on

GracieH: OMG gurlz. Tot DISASTER!!!

Charlotte: OMG WHAT?

GracieH: Cassie pulled hamstring!!!

KewlGrl82: No way! Um, who iz Cassie?

GracieH: R team's best forward!

Charlotte: Uh o! :O

GracieH: Ya, it happened @ practice 2-day.

Charlotte: Aw, Grace! :(

KewlGrl82: Can other ppl fill n 4 her?

GracieH: Well ya, but she iz best 1!!

Charlotte: :(

GracieH: Now r team will nev-r win!

KewlGrl82: Don't say that!

GracieH: But it's tru!

Charlotte: No way! U've been practicing so much. We've hardly seen u!

GracieH: Ya, but no Cassie meanz we aren't as good.

KewlGrl82: O u'll b fine!

GracieH: Thanks. :/ Sorry, got 2 go!

KewlGrl82: Ok, ttyl.

Charlotte: Me 2. C U 2-morrow gurlz!

GracieH: C U!

CHAPTER 9

Score One for Amy!

The rest of the week actually seemed to fly by with the speed of lightning, and before the English Roses knew it, it was Friday! Ah, glorious Friday. Just the word itself has a certain heavenly ring to it, doesn't it?

Amy had been spending every afternoon at the fashion show. There was only a week left until the big event, and Nigel was quite busy: choosing models, selecting outfits, auditioning hair and makeup artists, and more! Just watching Nigel sprint from one side of the room to the other was enough to make Amy dizzy!

Unfortunately, Amy seemed to botch every task he gave her. When he asked her to get him the Fall 2004 look books, she accidentally grabbed the Fall 2005 ones instead. When he asked for a spinach salad minus dressing, she thought he said *with* dressing. When he asked for all of the dangly earrings in the accessories department, she gave him simple studs. Now, Amy was not a stupid person. But it was as if all the common sense in her brain simply vanished whenever Nigel and his band of fashionistas were near. She felt almost as if they were just waiting for her to mess things up.

Because of these constant mishaps, Amy often
spent time with Simon. She would hand him tools
while he worked on different parts of the runway,
and listen to his dreams of someday opening his
own furniture store. Amy would stare dreamily at
him while he worked, and all the troubles of her
afternoons—the worries about Nigel, the stick
insects and their biting looks—would magically
vanish.

She told him all about her life, too: school; the strictness of her teacher, Mrs. Moss; and especially the English Roses. And Simon seemed to enjoy hearing Amy's stories about her life and school and friends just as much as she liked telling them!

"You remind me of my little sister," he remarked. Amy wanted to swoon.

Back to Friday, however! On this particular Friday, Amy was feeling restless. After all, her passion was fashion! She realized that she needed to show Nigel what she was really made of.

"Amy! Where is Amy?" Nigel called.

"I'm right here," Amy said in a clear voice.

"Oh," he said, seemingly startled. "I need the Juicy Couture headbands from accessories." He waved his hand as if to dismiss her.

"Certainly," she said, smiling. "And can I get you a latte?"

Nigel looked wary, apparently recalling Amy's last foray into the world of beverage preparation. "Well, um, okay. I suppose."

"Don't worry about a thing, Nigel," Amy called over her shoulder. "I've got it all under control."

i've got it all under control.....

#1 latte pour ↓

#2 juicy couture headbands ↘

Amy was in the kitchen, busily preparing the chai latte exactly as Winston had taught her a few days before (Charlotte's butler had come in handy with his foolproof recipe), when Nigel came waltzing in, a sour expression on his face.

"Amy, did you get those Juicy Couture hea—" He stopped short, then sniffed the air. His expression changed to one of bliss. "My, my, that smells... absolutely di-VINE!"

Amy winked. "Here, taste for yourself."

Nigel sipped the hot liquid, then closed his eyes. "Heavenly," he said.

"And those Juicy Couture headbands are right here," she added, handing him a bag filled with colorful headgear.

heavenly !!!

Nigel looked impressed. "Well, thank you!" He looked around the room, and his eyes fell on Amy's sketchbook, which was lying open on the table. He picked it up and began thumbing through the pages.

"Good," he murmured. "Quite good. Where did these come from?"

"Oh, I'm sorry," Amy apologized. "I know I'm not supposed to leave my stuff around, but I can't help but sketch while I'm waiting—"

Nigel looked up sharply. "These are yours?"

Amy wasn't sure what to say. "Well." She sighed. "Yes. Yes, they are."

"These are fantastic." Nigel was utterly fixated. "Astounding. You show much promise for a girl of your age. In fact, with this kind of talent, we could really use you more behind the scenes."

"Um, I don't know what to say, Nigel. I'm flattered."

"You should be, doll," Nigel said with a wink. "Now, follow me, and bring those headbands. There's much work to be done!"

CHAPTER 10

Who's That Girl?

drizz-zzle

The weekend flew by, as weekends are wont to do, and before they knew it, the English Roses were sailing along in Charlotte's Rolls Royce on their way to school. It was a gray and drizzly Monday, and by the time Royston (Charlotte's driver, can you imagine?) rolled up in front of Amy's house, the other Roses were already feeling that inherent sleepiness that seems to always come with drizzly Monday mornings.

But the sluggish mood in the car was completely blown away as soon as Amy flung open the door in a burst of chatty effervescence.

"Hi, girls! Isn't it a great day? I can't believe what a lovely spring day it is. I mean, sure it's raining, but you know what? There's something I love about spring rain. It just makes my curls stand out even more. And, ya know, Audrina? She's one of the fashion assistants working on the show? Well, she gave me this product that totally takes away frizz, even in rainy weather! Can you believe it? I can't."

Grace looked at her blankly. "What's your deal, girl?"

Amy looked confused. "Nothing! I just had a fabulous weekend, that's all!"

"Well, tell us all about it," Binah said, "'Cause we definitely need a pick-me-up."

"Well," Amy began, "I finally proved myself to Nigel. I made him a killer chai latte; and then he saw my fashion sketches, and he loved them!"

"That's great, Amy!" Nicole said. The rest of the English Roses nodded excitedly.

"Yeah," Amy said. "I know. So then I got to help dress some models and pick some accessories; and then Audrina and Paige, two of the fashion assistants, they took me shopping. It was sooo awesome." Amy examined her reflection in the window of the car. "In fact, Audrina told me that my lips are heart shaped. Don't you see it?"

The girls looked a bit baffled. "Heart shaped?" Grace said. "I guess so."

heart-shaped
LIPS

"Yeah. Heart-shaped lips are really great to have for close-ups. And Paige showed me these sit-up exercises that help you tone your abs. I did them all weekend, and I'm already beginning to see results. Just look at them!" She exposed her tummy. The other English Roses didn't see much of a difference.

For the rest of the ride to school, Amy gushed about her fabulous weekend with Audrina and Paige, and the rest of the Roses sat in silence.

After Royston had dropped the girls off in front of Hampstead, Amy stopped in front of a window to stare at her reflection. "Um, Amy," Nicole said impatiently, checking her watch. "We're going to

Introducing Simon Simmons

be late." All the Roses knew that Nicole hated to be one second late for class, especially on a Monday. She didn't like to miss anything!

"Not to mention, it's raining!" Charlotte squealed. "And my hair does get frizzy in the rain!"

"Yeah, I've been meaning to talk to you about that," Amy said as she whirled around to face Charlotte. "You really should use something to combat the frizz. I could give you a few tips."

Charlotte stared at her. "That's okay," she said tightly, and marched into the building, with Grace and Nicole following her. What was wrong with Amy? That kind of criticism didn't sound like her!

Amy shrugged and followed them inside.

But as the day wore on, things only got worse. In science class, Binah overheard Amy telling Ellie Richards that her teeth could use some whitening. At lunchtime, Amy turned to Grace. "You know, you really should put something on that zit. I have a product that will do just the trick!"

Grace gave her a look. "Don't even go there," she said, waving her hand.

"What?"

"You've been giving us nothing but fashion and beauty tips all day," Grace said.

"And what's with all the primping?" Charlotte asked. "Even I don't apply lipstick that often."

Amy was stunned. She truly thought the rest of the Roses would want to hear her beauty and fashion tips. "Sorry, guys," she said. "I didn't realize."

"It's okay," Binah said gently.

But inside, Amy couldn't help but be a bit annoyed. Why couldn't her friends be happy for her? She was finally living her dream!

CHAPTER 11

From Boring to Brilliant!

That afternoon, class seemed to drag on even more slowly than usual. Mrs. Moss, their strict sixth-grade teacher, didn't seem to grasp the fact that it's sometimes okay to make class fun instead of always being about rules, rules, rules! Their beloved fifth-grade teacher, Miss Fluffernutter, used to let them do fun things in class, such as bring in popcorn when they watched movies, or do art projects in history instead of answer boring questions in the back of their textbooks. But every teacher can't be Miss Fluffernutter quality; otherwise Miss Fluffernutter wouldn't be so very special!

Amy felt a poke in her back, and whirled around. The boy behind her passed her a note. Amy unfolded it. This is what it said:

We all know that Grace has been having a very hard time lately, with the tournament coming up. So I thought I'd hold a superspecial sleepover in her honor. Nigella is cooking Grace's favorite meal. Emma will do our hair and makeup, and I rented Grace's favorite movie, <u>Bend</u> <u>It</u> <u>Like</u> <u>Beckham.</u> Friday night, 8 p.m., my house. Be there!
Charlotte

Amy folded the note, and turned around to see Charlotte smiling. She gave her a thumbs-up. A sleepover was surely the best way to send Grace off to her big game in style.

CHAPTER 12

The Big Night... Before

A CHICKEN LEG

rom Monday to Tuesday to Wednesday to Thursday . . . and at last, it was Friday again—and a very special Friday, too, as it was the day before the big fashion show and Grace's football game; and the English Roses' big sleepover was scheduled for that very night! The girls were giddy with anticipation all day.

But while the rest of the Roses' heads were filled with visions of sleepovers and football games, Amy's was consumed with thoughts of fashion. The week had been a dream! She and Nigel were now like two peas in a pod; he consulted her on almost every decision he made, calling her his "fashion favorite." Audrina and Paige had become like Amy's big sisters, giving her constant advice on the colors and fabrics that were best suited to her.

The last bell finally rang, and the English Roses made plans to meet at Charlotte's by eight that evening. Amy threw on her jacket, grabbed her bag, and flew off to fashion show headquarters so quickly that you could almost see dust flying in her wake!

When she arrived, however, things were in general chaos. Nigel was running around breathlessly,

fanning himself worriedly. Audrina and Paige were clacking around after him, wringing their hands.

"What's the matter?" Amy asked breathlessly, running up to them.

"Oh dear. Things are not good," Nigel said. "Svetlana has food poisoning! She's in the hospital!"

"Oh no!" Amy cried. Svetlana was going to be wearing the biggest look—the final outfit! Secretly, what Amy was thinking, however, was, *Svetlana eats?* She was the tiniest model in the show!

"Yes," Audrina squealed. "We just don't know what to do!"

"No one else is available on such short notice," Paige added.

Amy didn't know what to say. How awful! All of the work they had been putting into the show, and now it would be short the best outfit of all (which Amy had helped put together). She squinched her face and pouted.

Nigel stared at her for a second, then narrowed his eyes. "Unless . . ." he began.

"Unless wh-a-a-at?" Audrina whined.

"Amy, darling!" Nigel gushed, taking Amy's hand. "Walk for me! Walk over there!"

Baffled, Amy walked to the center of the room and back.

"She'll need your expertise, of course," Nigel whispered to Audrina and Paige, who nodded enthusiastically.

"Could someone please tell me what's going on?" Amy asked, exasperated.

"Amy," Nigel began, eyes shining, "you will be our Svetlana for tomorrow's show."

"What?" Amy asked, confused. "What are you talking about?"

"You'll take her place, of course, silly!" Paige threw a tape measure around Amy's waist. "We'll need to get your measurements."

Amy felt her heart beating wildly. She was going to be a model!?

"Really? You want *me*?" She stared into the air dreamily, visions of herself as a high-fashion runway model dancing through her head. She thought of cute boys watching from the sideline,

Stella McCartney

perhaps throwing roses at her feet. She thought of Stella McCartney begging her to walk in her next show.

"Amy, dear," Audrina said. "We have much to do to get you ready for tomorrow. We have to perfect your runway strut and get your hair and makeup figured out."

Paige and Audrina rushed Amy out of the store. Amy felt as if she was walking on air! Amy Brook, a real fashion runway model.

One tiny thing seemed to be slipping her mind as she left, though. . . .

what was that ONE TINY THING...

???

CHAPTER 13

Work It, Girl!

"See," Amy said, "to walk like a real runway model, you have to step up first, like this."

"Wow." Amy's mum whistled. "Very impressive. You learned all this today?"

"Yeah." Amy shrugged. "Audrina and Paige taught me."

"What's this? Va-va-va-voom!" Amy didn't even notice that her stepdad, Richard, had walked into the room. She winced in embarrassment. Richard was just plain dorky, even though Amy was getting more used to him now that baby Stella was around.

Amy's eleven-year-old sister, Chloe, wandered in, too. "The English Roses called for you a bunch of times."

"What?" Amy was startled. Then she put her hand to her mouth. "Oh no!" she gasped. "The English Roses! Tonight was our sleepover!"

Amid all the modeling excitement, she had completely forgotten about her best friends! Of course, she had meant to call them as soon as she had heard the big news; but you know how even the most important things can slip your mind sometimes, especially when exhilaration takes hold!

"Mum, I have to go to Charlotte's right now!"

Amy's mother looked at her watch. "Absolutely not," she said. "It's way too late for you to be going out."

"But Mumsy," Amy whined.

"No arguing!" Amy's mum stated firmly. "My answer is no."

Amy didn't know what to do. She felt terrible about missing the big sleepover. She grabbed her cell phone. It was a little late to be making phone calls, but this was an emergency situation!

Charlotte's butler, Winston, answered on the first ring.

"Hi, Winston, it's Amy," she said breathlessly. "I really need to speak to the Roses. Are they there?"

"Terribly sorry," he said politely. "But Charlotte and the misses have retired for the evening."

"Oh," Amy whispered. Her heart sank. "Well, thanks anyway. Bye."

Amy hung up the phone feeling worse than she had when she had picked it up. Would the English Roses ever forgive her for missing a sleepover?

CHAPTER 14

Amy, Where Are You?

OH
NO
PT. 2

Amy tossed and turned throughout the
restless night. It seemed that every time
she fell asleep, something jerked her
awake; and then she would remember
how she had missed out on the sleepover, and a
horrible feeling of shame would creep over her.

A loud ringing at last woke her. She checked the
clock: 9 a.m. She picked up the phone.

"Amy, darling, where are you?" Nigel's shrill voice crackled on the other end of the line. "You need to get down here right away!"

"Oh, hi, Nigel," Amy said groggily, yawning sleepily. "What's going on?"

"We've got a fashion show in less than eight hours, and you need to get here ASAP," Nigel said in an exasperated tone.

"But . . . but I thought I didn't need to be there until six," she said.

"Well, that was before you were modeling in the show, darling," Nigel said impatiently. "Hair and makeup alone take four hours, and—"

"Nigel, I can't! It's my friend Grace's football game, and I have to be there for her. . . ."

"Football game?" Nigel icily repeated what Amy said as if she was speaking in another language. "I haven't a clue what you're talking about. The only thing I am absolutely sure of is this: If you want to be in this fashion show—in fact, if you want a career in fashion at all—you will get your sweet fanny down to this store PRONTO. That is all." There was a click as the other end went dead.

CHAPTER 15

Looking Good, Feeling Bad

our hours later, Amy was sitting in a chair in front of a brightly lit mirror while a man named Devonne held her eyelashes in a torture chamber.

"Argh!" Amy squirmed. "That eyelash curler hurts!"

"Sorry, dear," Devonne cooed. "Just twenty more seconds. We need your lashes to reach out into the audience."

Nigel hadn't been kidding. Getting her makeup done really had taken four hours. Well, two of those had been waiting, as Devonne's assistant had been late; and then Nigel hadn't liked the palette he had originally chosen, so Devonne had to start all over again.

All during the makeup session—an event that at any other time would have had Amy beside herself with excitement—Amy had been gnawing her

nails nervously. Getting her makeup professionally done just didn't seem right without telling the English Roses all about it. It almost was as if it wasn't happening at all.

Simon passed by and winked at Amy. "Looking good! What are you here so early for?"

"Oh, I didn't even get a chance to tell you!" she gushed. "One of the other models got food poisoning, so I'm going to be walking in her place."

"Well, well," Simon said with a smile. "Look who's the fashion plate, now? Congratulations." He frowned. "But wasn't today your friend's big football game?"

"Yes, today is Grace's game," she said sadly. "But Nigel said I had to be here or else I'd never work in fashion again."

"Did you try calling your friend and explaining the situation?" Simon asked.

"No," Amy said glumly.

"Hmm," Simon said. "That doesn't sound like the Amy I know."

Amy didn't know what to say. *She* didn't even know who she was anymore! The last two weeks of working on this fashion show had made her feel more confused than ever. She so badly wanted to work in fashion and to fit in with the cool crowd. But she also wanted to have space and time for her friends. Why couldn't she just have both?

"It also doesn't seem right that leaving for a few hours would ruin your fashion career forever," Simon reasoned. "I mean, you'll still be back in plenty of time for the show."

"That's true," Amy said.

Just then Audrina flitted by. "Amy," she cooed. "Nigel needs you in accessories—oh dear!" She seemed horrified.

"What?"

"Well, your hair color! It's just so . . . gingery. We need to do something about that right away." Audrina wrinkled her nose in disgust, then began playing with Amy's curls.

Taking a spin in Simon's convertible

Amy could feel her anger mounting. Her hair was her defining feature; it made her stand out from everyone else. And more than that, she *loved* it! Her shiny, scarlet curls were, well, just so unmistakeably *Amy*!

"Hmm," Audrina continued. "We'll try a weave, I think. Yes! Something blonde to soften your features a bit."

You could practically see smoke rising from Amy's head at this point, so incensed was she. A weave! The horror of putting some old, dirty, fake hair on top of her own; well, let's just say, the idea was less than pleasing.

Suddenly, Grace's words rang in Amy ears. *You're better than that.* And she realized she was.

"Thanks, Audrina," she said sweetly. "But I

don't think I'll be needing your help anymore."

Audrina just stood there, gaping. She didn't seem to know what to say.

Amy checked her watch. She still had some time!

"Now, if you'll excuse me," she hissed, "I have a football game to get to!"

CHAPTER 16

Rah, Rah, Roses!

The Walsham stadium was filled to capacity with cheering, screaming football fans. Hampstead and Walsham were battling it out on the field; but though Hampstead's team had given their all, Walsham was still leading by two goals. And there was only five minutes left in the game!

in the bleachers
(where's Amy???)

Let me tell you, dear reader, Grace was exhausted. Sweat dripped from her face, and her legs and cleats were caked with mud.

She looked up at the cheering crowd. She saw her family rooting for her, and, of course, the English Roses screaming their heads off, too. All except for Amy, that is. Grace shook her head, still in disbelief that Amy hadn't shown up for their sleepover last night OR for her game today. Well, wouldn't you have felt the same? It just didn't seem right that only four of the English Roses were there. As silly as it sounded, it felt as if only part of Grace was present on that football field. The absence of one best friend will do that, somehow.

Abby Weatherby dribbled the ball straight down the center of the field and gave it one of her signature power kicks. WHAM! The ball sank into the net.

"HAMPSTEAD GOAL!" the ref yelled. The crowd went wild.

Next, in a surprising move, Roberta Hamish stole the ball from Walsham's star forward and passed it to Grace. Grace dribbled it down to Walsham's goal and kicked it to Mary Poole, who looked as if she was going to give it back to Grace. Instead, though, she made a quick turnaround and maneuvered the ball past Walsham's goalie. The ball whooshed into the net.

The ref blew his whistle as the scoreboard changed to reflect the tied game. Walsham took a time out, and Grace joined her team in a huddle on the sideline.

As the coach barked orders and reviewed the plays that could give Hampstead their coveted win, Grace's eyes again drifted up to the bleachers.

TIME OUT!!!

And what she saw stunned her. For there, screaming her head off, was Amy! Red hair flying as she jumped in excitement, Amy was standing next to a handsome, older-looking boy; and both were holding up signs with words spelled out in huge black letters:

GO GRACE!

Grace caught Amy's eye and grinned. Amy gave her a huge thumbs-up. Suddenly, Grace knew she had what it took to give Hampstead their winning goal.

The ref called time in, and the players took the field. Grace narrowed her eyes at Walsham's forward, who gave her a menacing grin and shook her head.

The clock said that there were only sixty seconds left in the game. In a move that stunned even their coach, Grace chased after the ball at lightning speed. Walsham's forward was right there with her, but she deftly maneuvered the ball around her and kept right on running. Then, with one swift move of her ferocious foot, she kicked that ball straight into the net. And as the ref blew his whistle and the buzzer signaled the end of the game, the crowd simultaneously erupted into a frenzy, rushing the field.

Her parents and brothers ran up to her, covering her in kisses, hugs, and congratulations.

Suddenly, she was tackled from behind in a big bear hug—or rather, four big bear hugs!

"Congratulations, Gracie!" the English Roses—all of them, even Amy—chorused. "We knew you could do it!"

"Thanks, ladies." Grace grinned.

Amy stepped up. "I'm so sorry I missed the sleepover yesterday. After I found out I was going to be in the fashion show, my mind just sort of went blank, and—"

"Hold up. Wait a minute." Grace held up a hand. "You mean, you're going to be in the Teen Fashion Week runway show? Like a model?"

"Well, yeah. Gosh, I can't believe I haven't even told you guys yet. By the way, this is Simon."

Simon stuck out a hand. "Lovely to meet you all. I've heard so much about you."

Amy grinned. "Simon was nice enough to give me a ride over here from the fashion show."

Simon smiled at the Roses, flashing his perfect teeth. "No problem at all. Great match. Excellent goal, there, Grace."

All the Roses' tummies fluttered at the exact same time.

Charlotte checked her watch. "But isn't the show, like NOW?"

Amid all the excitement, Amy didn't realize how late it had gotten. The sun was already setting. She heaved a huge sigh. "I guess so. But I ran out of

Lovely to Meet You all....

there, and I don't think they'd want me in the show anymore."

Grace put her hands on Amy's shoulders. "No way. You are walking down that runway."

Charlotte nodded. "You have to at least try."

Simon checked his watch. "We've still got time. Come on, I'll give you a ride to the show, Simon-style!"

CHAPTER 17

Back in the Business!

The girls arrived at Marks & Spencer in Simon's 1965 red Mustang convertible. "Nice wheels!" Grace commented as she climbed out of the car.

"Thanks," Simon said. "I'll go park; you ladies get seats. I'll meet you inside!"

Amy took a deep breath and faced her friends. "I don't know if I'm ready for this."

Grace looked Amy straight in the eye. "Yes, you are! Go in there and strut your stuff already."

Amy realized Grace was right. She straightened her skirt, smoothed her curls, and marched into the store.

"Good luck, Amy," her friends called after her.

As soon as Amy entered the backstage area, she felt as if she had walked into another world. Models swarmed, bejeweled and decked to the nines in the latest fashions. Hair stylists and make-up artists rushed around the room, penciling in eyebrows and gluing together hair with styling gel, putting the last touches on their creations. Amid it all, Nigel could be heard screeching away, barking orders, and generally just being frantic.

Amy marched up to him and tapped him lightly

on the shoulder. "Nigel," she began, "I'd still like to walk in the fashion show tonight."

Nigel turned around and stared. "And just why should I let you? You just"—he flung his hand in the air dramatically—"ran off and totally shucked your responsibilities as part of this show!"

"Nigel, I know you think I flaked out on you," Amy said in a clear and confident tone. "And I'm sorry if I gave you the wrong impression about my

love of fashion. But today I had made a commitment to my friend, and I had to be there for her. What can I do to make you realize how serious I am about this? This, all of this"—she gestured around to the models and racks of clothes and general mayhem—"this is my *life!*"

Suddenly, a voice blared, "FIVE MINUTES TILL SHOWTIME."

Nigel paused, and narrowed his eyes. "Well, we *are* still short one model. Can you be through hair and makeup in five minutes?"

Amy grinned. "Can I? I'll show you how!"

CHAPTER 18

A Model Rose

front Row @ the
fashion Show

The lights dimmed in the auditorium as loud music pumped from speakers nearby. The English Roses, from their seats in the front row, visibly trembled with excitement as spotlights flashed overhead.

"Ladies and gentlemen," a loud voice boomed. "Welcome to the official Marks & Spencer Teen

Fashion Week. We've got some fashions hotter than a day at the beach for you today. Of course, all of these items are available in our New Attitudes department on the third floor. So now, without further ado, let the show begin!"

The music grew louder as models stepped out onto the catwalk, strutting their stuff in sun-kissed spring looks: playful jumpsuits, pretty floral print dresses, flowy silk skirts, brightly colored novelty T-shirts, gingham swimsuits, and dainty sandals.

Beach-wear!

"Where's Amy?" Grace hissed. "Maybe she didn't get to walk after all?"

No sooner had she spoken these words than Amy appeared from behind the curtain, decked out in a little floral dress with a flared skirt, silver high-heeled platform sandals, and a tan leather bucket bag. She paused, and the English Roses couldn't help but cheer and applaud at the sight of their friend.

At first Amy seemed a little unsure of herself on

the runway, but as soon as she heard the shrieks of the English Roses, her demeanor changed visibly. Her familiar, easy strut suited the catwalk perfectly; and once she reached the end, she did a perfect swivel, throwing a nonchalant hand on her hip to show off the little handbag. She sauntered back with complete confidence, tossing her head and turning around to wink at the audience, who broke into a round of applause.

Backstage, Amy was greeted by a beaming Nigel.

"You were phenomenal out there, Amy," he gushed.

"Thanks, Nigel," Amy said shyly.

"I have to apologize for my behavior over these past two weeks," Nigel said sheepishly. "Before any show I tend to get a bit of the . . . jitters."

"That's quite all right!" Amy replied.

"Any time you're available, you know I would love to have your savvy styling help around the store!" Nigel said.

Amy was so happy she felt as if her heart might explode right then and there. "I would be honored to help out after school sometimes." She grinned.

Soon, the English Roses met Amy backstage.

"Amy, you were to *die* for!" Charlotte exclaimed. "You look gorgeous."

"Your walk was so totally HOT!" Nicole added.

"You looked just like a real model up there," Binah said.

AMAZING!!!

HOT!!!

PHENOMENAL!!!

"Only better." Grace finished.

"Much better" came a deep voice from behind them. The English Roses whirled around to find Simon smiling his beautiful, deep, genuine smile and holding a bouquet of daisies.

"Um, Amy, I think we're going to—uh—go check out those racks of clothes over there," Charlotte said with a wink, ushering the rest of the Roses away.

wonderful!!

"These are for you, Amy," Simon said, his eyes sparkling.

"Wow, thanks," Amy replied. Her mouth suddenly went dry as a desert, and she found herself at a loss for words.

"You looked great, too," he added. "It's cool to see a normal-looking girl modeling clothes. Those super-skinny models look sorta sick." He wrinkled his nose.

"Yeah," Amy agreed. "I wish all models looked like normal girls instead of stick-thin insects."

"You're a sweet kid," Simon told her. "Keep in touch, okay?"

Amy smiled. "Definitely!"

Then Simon leaned over and kissed Amy on the cheek! And if she thought her heart was going to explode before, right then it felt like a rocket ship that had just taken off for the moon.

Just then the English Roses returned with their arms full of clothes.

"Nigel is totally a peach!" Charlotte exclaimed.

"He let us have all these clothes for free!" Binah said happily.

As the girls showed one another their spiffy new duds, Amy took a whiff of the daisies in her arms.

Yeah, she thought, *I could definitely get used to a career in fashion.*

MADONNA RITCHIE was born in Bay City, Michigan, and now lives in London and Los Angeles with her husband, movie director Guy Ritchie, and her children, Lola, Rocco, and David. She has recorded 18 albums and appeared in 18 movies. This is the ninth in her series of chapter books. She has also written six picture books for children, starting with the international bestseller *The English Roses*, which was released in 40 languages and more than 100 countries.

JEFFREY FULVIMARI was born in Akron, Ohio. He started coloring when he was two, and has never stopped. Soon after graduating from The Cooper Union in New York City, he began drawing for magazines and television commercials around the globe. He currently lives in a log cabin in upstate New York, and is happiest when surrounded by stacks of paper and magic markers.